# Power Magazine

## Issue 9

First published January 2022 by Fly on the Wall Press
Published in the UK by
Fly on the Wall Press
56 High Lea Rd
New Mills
Derbyshire
SK22 3DP

www.flyonthewallpress.co.uk
ISBN: 978-1-913211-71-4
Copyright remains with individual authors © 2022

The right of the individual authors to be identified as the authors of their work has been asserted in accordance with the Copyright, Designs and Patents Act 1988.

Edited by Isabelle Kenyon and Olivia Katrandjian. Typesetting by Isabelle Kenyon. Cover photo Unsplash.

All rights reserved. No part of this publication may be reproduced, stored in or introduced into a retrieval system, or transmitted in any form, or by any means (electronic, mechanical, photocopying, recording or otherwise) without prior written permissions of the publisher. Any person who does any unauthorised act in relation to this publication may be liable for criminal prosecution and civil claims for damages.

A CIP Catalogue record for this book is available from the British Library.

# Contents

| | |
|---|---|
| Home Office Property by **Rachel Burns** | 5 |
| Derelict Seminary by **Rachel Burns** | 6 |
| The Man of Many Masks by **Kate Young** | 7 |
| Uluru-Kata-Tjuta National Park by **Kate Young** | 8 |
| Aftermath by **Jane Ayres** | 9 |
| The Politics of Pain by **Jane Ayres** | 10 |
| The pet by **Jane Ayres** | 11 |
| Artworks Evergreen and In Strength by **Eunice Ukamaka** | 12-13 |
| Cue the Fish Palace by **Selma Carvalho** | 14 |
| Artworks Geothermal Power and Haulbowline Lighthouse Power by **John Winder** | 19 |
| Coal to ashes by **Bonnie Meekums** | 20 |
| On point by **Bonnie Meekums** | 22 |
| one thousand leucotomies by **Alex Reed** | 23 |
| In the District of Eden by **Alex Reed** | 24 |
| Sovereign Fruit by **Michael Conley** | 25 |
| Constitution by **Michael Conley** | 26 |
| *"You have been told so many lies..."* by **Tim Kiely** | 27 |
| Beyond the Polished Table by **Maggie Veness** | 28 |
| The Hand of a Writer by **Sarah-Jane Crowson** | 31 |
| Emptying Las Vegas by **Marie Papier** | 32 |
| Gale by **Marie Papier** | 33 |
| Intruders by **Desree** | 34 |
| Oddjob by **Desree** | 35 |
| Zarmina's baby by **Maria FitzGerald** | 36 |
| They say I am the firstborn by **Martins Deep** | 37 |
| Catharsis by **Martins Deep** | 39 |
| Genesis 1:3 by **Joe Williams** | 40 |
| Part Time Anarchist by **Joe Williams** | 41 |
| The Politician by **Bill Lythgoe** | 42 |
| Secrets of a cartographer's wife by **Katrina Dybzynska** | 44 |
| The Dictator's Wife watching ships by **Katrina Dybzynska** | 45 |
| [superpower vs sinopower] by **Yuan Changming** | 46 |
| [the greatest soft power: for qi hong] by **Yuan Changming** | 47 |
| doubt is our product by **Nick Allen** | 48 |
| Community Service by **Carter Lappin** | 49 |
| The Bees by **Julie Stevens** | 50 |
| Artwork Woman by **Charlotte Jung** | 51 |
| You Can't Always Get the Stains Out by **Jennifer Rowe** | 52 |
| Fish by **Eve Chancellor** | 55 |

| | |
|---|---|
| The Date by **Kevin Crowe** | **57** |
| Rubble (The Demolished People) by **Thomas Lawrance** | **58** |
| Passing a statue of a lion hunting a gazelle in Victoria by **Christian Ward** | **59** |
| Two artworks by **Despy Boutris** | **60-61** |
| Review of 'Things I Have Forgotten Before' by Tanatsei Gambura, published by Bad Betty Press by **Tim Kiely** | **62** |

# Home Office Property
**Rachel Burns**

*Beware Prison Dog Patrol*
 *Keep Out*

The concrete perimeter
lights up sepsis yellow
like a scene
on a cutting room floor,
if hell had high security walls.

The east wind whips
gravel from the one-track road
shakes dog shit bags from trees
like loose pennies.

I slip between the sycamores
into the nature reserve;
walk the figure eight
around the two lakes.

Spent gun cartridges
bob to the surface
dislodged by the thaw,
swans scatter across the lake
like funeral confetti,

and a mute
flanks the wooden footbridge
like he is on guard
black splayed feet
white puffed-out chest,
curved neck.

# Derelict Seminary
**Rachel Burns**

Someone steps on broken glass;
the sound shakes the wood pigeons
from the sycamores.
In the school yard, yellow loosestrife
grows in the fissures of asphalt.

We trace the razor wire fence
ignoring warning signs
*Police Dog Training Area*
past used condoms
and dead man bottles.

Inside the junior chapel, stained glass
greets us in the window's yawn.
One of us throws the first brick.
We all join in. The noise
stone breaking glass
the high octave notes
of lost boys, a hallelujah
torn from the throat in the dark.

Spent, we sit on paving flags,
our breath halos in the stained-glass silence.
The broken window of the chapel
a child's kaleidoscope
you can't twist into shapes
or bear to look through, anymore.

# The Man of Many Masks
**Kate Young**

She wakes early and wonders which face he will wear today. If she is lucky, he will pull the pale grey stretch of skin across his cheek bones, for this will allow laughter lines to crinkle at the edges of his eyes, his lips to curl into elastic kindness.

heads turn, catch her smile
as she glides the nave slowly
falls into his heart

Some mornings she rolls into the darkness spread across the bed. She hardly recognises this man, features set as if caked in corrugated cardboard and she knows to slip into the shadows of the day.

when she looks closely
she can see the signs she missed
or chose to ignore

On 'in-between-the-mood' days, they walk hand-in-hand between shaded trees and pause to admire the bluebells, their little cupped mouths open as if announcing spring's tune. She listens to the feathered ripple of blackbird song but knows he hears a different sound.

violins play Bach
repeated conversations
littering the air

She often feels as if she has slipped into a Shakespearean tragedy, unsure of this granite man she simply thought was Mercurial, his winged feet nimble as quicksilver. Lately, he has become static, a statue made of marble, but still she is fixated by his polish and charm.

granite is heavy
and she is too weak to lift it
from the face she loves

# Uluru-Kata-Tjuta National Park
## Kate Young

We follow the flat tarmac curve.
Giant-headed domes rise,
molars cast on a monolithic mass
cavernous in the slump of sun.

I sense the creep of awe,
its buzz and hum a magnet
as I scramble over scrapes
of shouldered granite, basalt.

Covered in carmine dust,
my face, my throat
is a swallow of sandstone
as I lift from base to summit.

A swarm of freckles
appear on the ridge
like last summer's ants,
a scribble on terracotta

leaving their trace
in the deepest of shadows.
The scrawl of a path,
snakes like breath

and Mount Olga yawns.
A ravine appears;
water pools at the foot of a gorge,
sighs over cobbles and myth.

# Aftermath
## Jane Ayres

Take a china mug
Add 1 heaped teaspoon of cocoa powder (pure, unsweetened)
A teaspoon of instant coffee
Notice how easily it dissolves in boiling water
Tendrils of steam a reminder
Fill a china jug with milk (full cream)
Half a teaspoon of cinnamon
No sugar
Never sugar
Place in microwave – two minutes should do –
But you may have to add a further 20 seconds
Since the microwave has a mind of its own
Watch and wait
Anticipate that frothy, lactose caffeine fix
Ping!
Pour bubbles of milk into the mug
Stir (it always needs a lot of stirring)
Wrap your scarred hands around the hot china
Press hard
Harder
Until it burns already blistered fingertips
The smell of searing flesh
A reminder
The sizzle of his voice
A clusterfuck of sugarsweet honey & blood
You tremble
You are safe now
If only you could believe it

# The Politics of Pain
Jane Ayres

### The parent

The zebra-striped uniform of the Macmillan nurse represents defeat, betrayal.
    *Not everyone has a good relationship with morphine*
You hate the way it makes you feel sick, disoriented,
weighing this against being sentient, but in pain.
    You opt for the latter.

When you decide to give up, your tell-tale heart,
programmed for survival, keeps pumping, thumping.
Death will be slow – agonising starvation, dehydration, organ failure. I can give you nothing,
to ease this suffering. I can do nothing.

    I can do nothing.

*She hasn't long. A day. Two.*
We keep vigil by your hospital bed for seven long nights.
*Talk to her. She can hear you.* Can she? How do you know?

Surreal: witnessing dying.
We become characters, the cruel inevitability unlike any rose-tinted drama.
We, your children, are helpless. We stay. We keep watch.

    We keep watch.

The nurse returns once, twice –
after I plead for the attention you need.
She offers dampened cotton wool
to moisten your paper-dry lips.

You did the same for your sister in her final days, my child-self wondering
if I would have your strength when the time came.

*She died peacefully* – the familiar, sugar-coated lie.
*No, she didn't,* I reply but no-one wants to hear.
Rage splinters, shards lodging forever in my honeycombed heart.

**The pet**

*He's had a happy life. Twelve is good in cat years*, the vet assures us. *After the sedative, he will simply slip gently away, without pain.*

    A good ending.

# Evergreen
**Eunice Ukamaka**

# In Strength
## Eunice Ukamaka

# Cue the Fish Palace
**Selma Carvalho**

I was at the Fish Palace watching goldfish in their glass containments dart through tangles of plastic seaweed, when it occurred to me that they couldn't help themselves — the goldfish had some inner sense directing them into movement which, if not bizarre, was utterly without purpose. It was lunchtime and the restaurant was deserted. Harry, the owner, came and sat with me. I told him about what had happened on the M4.

—The thing is, Harry, I was waiting for the signal to turn, and the woman in the next lane cut me off. Naturally, I followed her white sedan for some distance, and when I finally caught up with her, I yelled at her. One would think she'd show some contrition.

That's what I was hoping for: an act of contrition that would prove she was aware she'd made a mistake. I would then drive off without giving the incident further thought. Instead, the woman threw the apple she'd half-eaten at my car and drove off laughing. It was at this precise moment, as the yellowed remains of fruit came flying in my direction, I felt the collapse of civilisation as we know it; for if it didn't exist within us to show repentance when clearly one had erred, then human society was on a slippery slope to hell. I said as much to Harry.

Harry looked at me with intense eyes. He was always aroused by the stories I told him, perhaps because Harry suffered the sort of alienation long working hours enforced on him. He'd given up on exploring the neighbourhood, and instead sifted through these stories with great interest, provided opinion and moral context, so that the stories became hyperbole. Together, we'd pontificate about the world and feel better about ourselves. I realised it was important to be appreciative of this contemplation, but I sensed Harry had retired to it prematurely. For he still wanted, in some manner, to experience the world more fully. He had pushed aside those ambitions for now and was instead feeding off outrage or joy siphoned off other people.

Harry signalled to Marie and she came over with the menu. Harry watched her lantern face while I ordered a prawn pil pil. For sure, Harry had often wanted to ask her out, but for whatsoever reason refrained. In fact, I'd not seen Harry with a woman in the two months I'd known him; perhaps he's meeting his needs in some synthetic way, I thought, but I'd never felt brave enough to ask him. Our relationship did not afford us that sort of intimacy. In many ways, our relationship too felt inorganic. It relied entirely on documenting the present, it existed within the restaurant, without a past or a future. We were denied the kind of friendship that comes with longevity, which has the ability to mould people's sense of self, fluctuating between kindness and cruelty and arriving eventually at what one considers to be the core of the person. That sense of our essential selves did not exist between Harry and me, although in every other way, it felt like a real friendship. At times, the intensity with which we shared the everyday felt so unique that it surpassed the warmth that comes with a historical understanding of the other person.

Harry sat in the dim light, and leaning forward, said:
—Describe her to me, the woman who cut you off.

She was middle-aged, and other than that I couldn't give Harry any more details, but what I recalled with clarity was the sticker she had stuck to her car, advertising the Hag's Head.

—By God, said Harry, 'I know the woman.' She owned the Hags Head pub and came in often for jellied eels. Harry was thrilled that he was connected, however peripherally, to the story.

—The next time she comes in, I won't serve her. I'll simply say, we don't serve your kind here. No doubt, she'll ask me what kind that is, and I'll have great pleasure in saying, fascists.

Harry had done what he was rarely able to do; he had inserted himself into the story, he had taken action to impact its outcome. I felt a weight lift off me, like a great moral dilemma had been resolved, like the equilibrium on the planet had been restored by this one act. Harry became an avenger; whatever smallness I'd felt when that apple hit my car was washed away. Sitting at the Fish Palace, I felt once again the need to celebrate life, to believe in its goodness, to believe in the righteousness of people.

As Harry served the one other customer in the restaurant, he seemed illumined by a special light. His side-burns, which usually proved to be a distraction to fully appreciating his face, now seemed an integral part to understanding the essence of the man. The aquiline nose, the deep-set eyes, the fleshy mouth—Harry was much more handsome than I'd given him credit for. Were it not for the fact that he was at least twenty years older than me, and much more importantly that I'd committed myself to a life of twenty-something promiscuity, I might well have considered Harry as a candidate for the father of my children. Whatever progeny we produced would go on being righteous like their father. The more I observed Harry, the more upright he seemed, and I wanted to belong in some measure to the aura he exuded. Harry that day looked altogether heraldic.

It was a quiet afternoon as London often is between winter and spring when rain threatens, greying the sky, but doesn't always arrive; those days of quietude lend themselves to contemplative pursuits; I pulled out a book by Carol Ann Duffy as I waited for James to arrive. James and I had known each other forever, and felt the sort of attraction coupled with familiarity which allowed us to sleep with each other without necessarily feeling the need to commit to anything deeper. This thing I had with James was the only permanence I encountered in my life, and even though James now lived in Manchester and only occasionally visited London, I felt with him what expansiveness in friendship allows people to feel, a rootedness in their own being, a definition of themselves which goes back to a time when they might have been entirely different people, and the possibility that they'd know each other for long enough to grow into someone else. James was shorthand for understanding my life, giving it more solidity than it seemed to have to its composition on most days.

The restaurant was unusually quiet, as I told James what had happened earlier, and the heroic promise Harry had made. James, never one to lose an opportunity, immediately tweeted about Harry's goodness, and instantly had two likes. The world approved. In an hour, at which point we had both finished our main course of prawn pasta for me and grilled squid for James, he had fifty likes. The world's approval kept growing. I smiled at James. James too was part of Harry's goodness. Or, at the very least James wanted to spread Harry's goodness. If we just kept going, if we just kept multiplying the goodness quite clearly being generated at the Fish Palace, then we could change the world. The thin March air blew into the Fish Palace just then, carrying the smell of fish to our table. I noticed with some agitation fish of various type placed on ice in the kitchen, salmon, trout and sea bream, nausea welling in my throat.

James and I went back to my place. He was staying for a month this time. Over the years, our agreement had become tacit. So deeply were we attuned to each other that like dolphins, we could intuit each other's needs. If it was likely that I was not predisposed to having sex with James that day, James would know, and he would make no more of it. He would simply settle himself on the sofa with a duvet from the linen closet, and say, right, I'm here for the night. Perhaps arousal has a special smell to it, or more likely, an urgency to it, which no amount of evolution can dent, and our baser selves can feel that frisson, that small tear in ourselves which so desperately needs mending; that desire to dive into our physical selves and wrench from it whatever needs wrenching, like detritus at the bottom of a garden pond, which lies there, and just needs cleaning once in a while. I felt wretched thinking of all the things humans had ceded to evolution, and produced instead politeness and politics and conurbations of concrete which made of us all automatons. But intimacy and our need for it was something evolution couldn't rid us of.

That night, James did not make love to me. He should have known I desperately wanted to, but he didn't. This withholding, I considered to be a terrible meanness. I had no idea why it had occurred, only that it had. I sensed something opaque and ambivalent stirring in him.

James did not sleep with me the entire week; I missed him deeply, but I said nothing. I stopped by at the Fish Palace. Harry had stuck a poster on his windowpane which read: *No profanity, No abuse*. It was mid-morning and the restaurant was not open yet. Harry motioned to me to come in. I saw at once that he was preoccupied with a woman in the far corner. The woman was large and badly dressed. Despite being quite a distance away, her weepy voice carried through the confined space, although I could not discern the words. When the woman finally left, Harry came over to where I sat. I didn't want to pry, so I avoided asking him what that was all about, but Harry felt the need to confide in me. The woman was being persecuted by a neighbour.

—How?

—All manner of things: overgrown trees, noise at odd hours, cats camping in her garden.

It so happened, three years ago, the neighbour had ordered Persian caviar from the Fish Palace for a dinner party, but when it arrived it was several days past expiry. The neighbour had taken possession of it anyway, and told Harry that it was fine when he served it later that night. Harry was going to make public this knowledge.

I stared at Harry blank-eyed. I was uncomfortable with what he was proposing: using the neighbour's past and his knowledge of it against him. The alchemy of human contract was being altered here: shouldn't the neighbour be allowed the privacy of his past life? Why should anyone wade through muck and emerge with the dregs of our former selves?

—No one arrives in this world fully formed. In denying that man forgiveness, you are denying him the possibility of redemption. Where's your compassion, Harry?

My unwillingness to cheer Harry on caught him off-guard. After all, it was I who initiated this 'movement', and in some respect, I suppose, he saw me as its prophet. I softened my tone, and touching his hand gently, said, I'm sure you know what you're doing, Harry, I trust you. There's no one else I trust more than you. I know you're always going to be on the right side of my conscience. I had to believe that about Harry, that in the balance, he would act judiciously. I convinced myself the neighbour had put the lives of his dinner guests at risk, and had to be punished for this offence.

A crowd was beginning to crown the glass door now.

—This is all good for business. He laughed excitedly. A strong smell of fish clung to him, and I was glad when at last he put some distance between us. When I got home, James had his laptop open, but he shut it as soon as he saw me.

—Who was that?

—Who?

I'd heard the voice of a man, a deep, gravelly voice that carried obvious authority. After a pause, James said:

—You wouldn't understand.

—Who is he? I insisted.

—A man with unpopular ideas.

The barrier between James and me, which until then had been a thin film, thickened to something more solid. How could I be incapable of understanding a thought? Perhaps, I wouldn't approve was more accurate, for thoughts are not beyond comprehension and certainly between friends who are sometimes lovers, the precise role of thoughts is communal dissection. Perhaps this man was the reason James was no longer sleeping with me. Perhaps this man had insinuated an idea so perverse in James' mind that it made my body and the acts it engaged in foul or immoral. I was no longer the owner of my body, its boundaries were no longer decided by me but by some force outside of my being—a force James was convinced was beyond my comprehension, a force possibly so polar to everything I stood for that the gap was unbridgeable. And yet, a force so powerful that it decided who would or would not be the recipient of my most intimate self. An overwhelming loneliness swept through me, and a type of derangement which I'd not experienced until then. If I could not affect the course of my relationship with James, if James was now under the influence of a sinister talking-head on YouTube, then here indeed was the abject dissolution of the self.

I watched James' lank body sprawled on the sofa and I wanted it all the more. I came to despise this unknown man, replacing our shared childhood, our fumbling adolescence, our unfulfilled early adulthood, with his own version of our lives together, his falsehoods about who I was as a person. He was taking James away from me precisely when it was beyond my endurance to bear such a loss. That night, the rain was savage as it lashed fiercely at the roof and at the small garden I had been tending to; plants were ripped from their roots and strewn across the inadequate podium. The rain bruised everything, arriving in an unstoppable torrent. James continued to listen to the man on YouTube. I tried to talk to him, but he stared at me vacantly. He left the next morning, cutting short his stay in London, and returned to Manchester.

Occasionally, I receive an email from him or a like on my Facebook and Twitter pages, but our lives, the ones we had before the man of the LCD monitor made his appearance, are gone. In another version of this ending, we email frequently, visiting often our earlier lives, trying to find common ground. Despite the unreliability of our recollections, some things have held, things that reside within us and can't be erased, like our humour, our love of good books and music festivals, the memory of nights when we fully appreciated the transitory nature of life and its pleasures.

A month passed, and I went to the Fish Palace. The place was heaving. I had to wait at the bar for quite some time before Marie came over and led me to a table. She looked more beautiful than ever, earthy in a manner few women choose to look these days. There was no pretence about her, no shying away from the largeness of her body. Instead, Marie had fully embraced her enormous breasts and buttocks, embraced her body for what it could be on cold winter nights—a receptacle of joy, a column of flesh for men to thrust into until they screamed into nothingness. The only thing that felt unpolluted at the Fish Palace was Marie. I was glad that Harry had never asked her out and defiled her with his fish breath.

    From where I sat I could see the fish slabbed in the kitchen, most gutted and filleted, but there were some still left whole and wide-mouthed, as if their lives had been extinguished mid-breath. The smell of fish permeated the airless restaurant but everyone dined unmindful of it. Harry came and sat with me for a while, his skin withered like seaweed, his hair silvered with fish scales, and his mouth one giant gill, flapping endlessly. Harry, I knew, conjugated life through fish. That's what he knew about the world, the value of fish. It was the last time I would see Harry. Whatever else I would become in life, I could not become this.

# Geothermal Power and Haulbowline Lighthouse Power
John Winder

# Coal to Ashes
**Bonnie Meekums**

Edith Sykes kneels on the bare stone, tucking her apron under swollen knees. These days, raking the fire is difficult, getting up harder. She reaches for the hearth brush. Leaning forward, she begins her early morning ritual of coaxing soot down the chimney. There's little feeling in her hands, but they've done this job a thousand times. They complete the task like a released wind-up toy.

Edith pulls out the tray, then reaches for her ash pan. Thomas's brother nickel plated it himself, as a wedding gift. Once more her red hands set to work, sweeping up every last bit of ash and pouring it into the tray. Waste not, want not.

She shifts her weight onto one knee, gripping the tray in her stronger hand as she reaches forward with the other to steady herself on the chimney. She winces from the pain of bone on stone as she releases her knee and slides her foot forward. Then, with a push on foot and chimney, she is up. She allows herself the shadow of a smile. Not one speck of ash has spilled.

Once outside, a sudden gust slams the door shut behind her, as flying ash stings her eyes. Edith mutters a gentle oath, her vision blurred. She feels her way down the icy path laying the remnants of last night's fire, eking it out to the garden gate. No-one will slip on her path. She pauses to blink, refocussing her eyes to scan the distance. The mine stands like a dinosaur on the horizon. She tries to picture the men underground. She's never been down, but she's heard the local lads describe it often enough. Colliers to a man. They tell tales of daily dangers and heroics, no doubt embroidered more elaborately than their mothers' samplers in the hope of impressing a girl. Sometimes, the men speak in hushed voices that are not for women's ears.

Today is her lad Joseph's first day. At fourteen, it's time to be a man. Time to go crawling on hands and knees into tight spaces the older men can no longer squeeze in, though once they did. Joseph is strong but wiry. His lungs are not yet black. He will be called upon to set the charge. Edith pulls her shawl tightly around her shoulders. Thomas will be there. He will look out for his boy.

Edith turns back up the path. Once inside, she lays the hearth with yesterday's coal, then kindling, then she adds coiled newspaper, taking special care to shape it into an image of the trumpet Joseph will now play in the colliery band. She adds more kindling, wood split by her husband, and finally fresh coal. All ready to light for her men. Men. So strange to think of her little boy as a man. Edith's nipples tingle involuntarily as she remembers him, so small and needy, born too soon. She knew instinctively to tuck her miniature baby into her dress, his little body nestling against her skin. She wraps her already-tight shawl a little tighter, crossing it over and tucking the ends into her apron as she remembers that day.

She wasn't ready to let him out into the world. The midwife gave Edith a pitying look but said nothing. The doctor said the child wouldn't live and left her to it.

'Let her do what she must,' he advised the midwife, as he shook his head.

Edith never managed to keep a second pregnancy long enough to have another baby to hold and feed. Joseph was her gift from the angels.

Edith is glad of the housework today. She sings the song her Welsh cousin taught her when she was a girl, *Cwm Rondda*, as she works the dough, thudding it down like a potter at her wheel, then folding and repeating in an easy, soothing rhythm. At one point she hears a rumble in the distance, like the heavens joining in. Edith smiles at the thought, despite her quickening heartbeat.

It's long after dark, the stew bubbling on the range, fresh bread and butter ready on the kitchen table when Edith finally hears footsteps crunch up the ashes on her path. Her ears burn as she checks there are two sets. She hardly recognises her son's gait; already, her boy sounds like a grown man.

The door opens, the fire in the grate dancing like a giddy child. Her husband stands in the doorway, cap in hand. Edith peers around him, anxious to quiz her boy about his first day as a man. But behind Thomas, Edith can just make out the outline of the manager. Her husband's eyes search hers. His bottom lip quivers.

Edith's own eyes sting for the second time today. She looks at the fire, blazing in her tidy grate, and grips her shawl.

# On point
**Bonnie Meekums**

CW / TW: Sexual abuse, murder

My feet screamed, but I kept on smiling. The director, Hernando, was known for shouting at dancers to get out, his forefinger aimed like a knife towards the door, threatening at any moment to cut our dreams to shreds. We all would stay motionless in silent solidarity when it happened, waiting for his roar to end, the tension to subside. Until the next time. He wanted aesthetic motion, not human beings with feelings and frailties.

I was lucky to be here. Having started late, teachers tried to warn me off.

'You want to be a dancer, do you?' Practised condescension kicking me in the guts. Holding my stomach, I laced up my shoes, danced and bled, but artistic directors looked over my head, smiling encouragement at the girls who'd first donned pink satin while still in nappies. When they reached puberty, chest buds threatening boyish figures, those same girls pushed peas around plates, hid meals in dogs. They got the jobs, praised for how light they were – how easy to lift, as if dancing required no corporeality, no steely strength.

But then along came Hernando with his love of flesh, and I was propelled into his dance company. The offer came with certain expectations. He saw it as his contractual right to slide his swollen hands over our flesh, all the while applauded by dance critics, hailed as a feminist because he wasn't like the others who demanded anorexia as a meal ticket. At the end of each show he could be found behind the curtains, his cock thrusting in and out of a different dancer each day, and two on Sundays. There were eight of us. He liked to be fair.

'Eh, gringa!' He tapped his stick loudly on the bare, wooden floor, bringing me back with a jolt to the pain in my bones. I muttered 'no soy gringa, soy Inglesa' under my breath, a familiar incantation as he strode towards me.

'Yes, Hernando,' I said aloud, eyes to the ground. He liked it like that. It turned him on, stopped him getting nasty.

'Keep that big arse tucked in,' he said, patting my behind, an oily smile creeping over thin lips.

Sometimes, a quick fuck behind the curtains wasn't enough. He had to take one of his harem home. That's when I would have to perform for him.

'Come on! You can dance! Show me what you got!'

I learned to do a coquettish strip, writhing and teasing, all the while thinking of the moment it would be over. It's easier, when you kid yourself you're in charge. Easier than waiting, eyes and ears alert, breath held.

One steamy summer's evening I told Hernando I had a special treat prepared, to celebrate two years with his company. With each clothing layer removed, I spooned a different salmagundi onto his tongue – huevos motuleños, arroz a la tumbada, chiles en nogada – each taste growing stronger as he drooled, his cock growing bigger.

Then I mounted him, still wearing a thick, studded leather belt that accentuated my hips. He moaned, clutching my breasts.

As he climaxed I reached around my back and removed the slender blade I'd hidden there.

When I plunged it into his heart, his screams answered the call of my battered bones.

# one thousand leucotomies
## Alex Reed

the approach to the brain is through a trephine hole
in the skull made under local or general anaesthetic

through the opening an instrument is introduced
& moved so that it cuts white matter

a cutting of the white matter
the white conducting fibres
the particular fibres

known as the pre-fronto thalamic tract
connecting the pre-frontal area
of the frontal lobe

with the thalamus
the pre-frontal or forward part
concerned with thought

the thalamus has functions
concerned with feeling
the precise functions are obscure

a portion of the thalamus-nucleus medialis dorsalis
degenerates when the fronto-thalamic fibres have been cut
right & left can be dealt with in one session

the purpose is to break
the connection between thoughts & emotions
take the sting from experience

if all goes well she ceases to care & is thus freed

*This poem includes text drawn from, Pre-Frontal Leucotomy in 1,000 Cases. Board of Control, (England & Wales, 1947).*

# In the District of Eden
**Alex Reed**

125 YEARS AGO:
BODY FOUND: The frozen body of a lunatic who escaped from the Alston Workhouse was found on Haresceugh Fell.
*Hexham Courant*, 9th February 2018.

Mother must've known I'd come
here where they'll never catch me
she's set a place where I can rest
a bed of stones for shelter

By this broken wall she's left
a sheep's skull for company
which speaks to me in my Father's voice
under stars as bright as heaven

# Sovereign Fruit
**Michael Conley**

Another new obsession: this time it's peaches. He loves peaches so much He's renamed them 'Sovereign Fruit' and has decreed that nobody else is allowed them but Him, like he did with chicken nuggets last year.

Not only that, but every time He eats one now, He insists upon an audience of at least six of us, seated before Him on uncomfortable plastic chairs.

He grips it like an Australian spin bowler, and first runs the tip of His nose, then the tip of His tongue, all the way up and down the peach's arse-crack, one eye closed in delectation, the other checking His audience is paying close enough attention.

Yes, of course He chews with his mouth wide open: that first bite in the silence of the room sounds like the slow removal of a child's wellington boot from a deep tub of wallpaper paste.

For someone who loves eating peaches so much, there are, in fact, two things He hates about eating peaches. The first is touching the slimy orange flesh with His fingers. The second is the idea of His front teeth finding the harsh resistance of the peach pit. Both of these sensations make him want to puke, he says.

After the first bite, then, He hands the peach over to a white-gloved valet, who rotates it, keeping stone always a safe distance from bite. These bites are more delicate than the first, like the sound of a Labrador snuffling at the testicles of another Labrador. The very best peach-rotators can work it so that the stone ends up completely bald. The very worst peach-rotators remain in exile.

When He has finished, He stands and bows, waits for the thunderous applause to subside and announces, proud as a new father, "SOVEREIGN FRUIT."

The audience is dispersed and the peach pit buried in the Legislatorial Arboretum.

Since the first reports of unrest in the provinces, He has started doing this two or three times a day.

# Constitution
## Michael Conley

Difficult to decide whether His new obsession is better or worse than the old one, really. We're split on it, as usual. Here it is, an ancient law He has discovered, one of those that are still unaccountably on the statute books:

*the monarch may discharge his musket into the torso of any male serf of marriageable age*

*and furthermore the monarch may do this once daily with the exception of the Sabbath and other public holidays*

He doesn't read, so how has He found this? It's so on-brand it could've been written for Him. His face when He saw it! Licking His lips like an old ham pantomiming big bad wolf.

He's added His own amendments in what looks like black crayon:

*and furthermore the shooting will take place on the Palace roof, with the monarch standing on the helipad and the serf standing on the edge of the roof and a large pile of fresh horse manure at the bottom for the dead serf to fall headfirst into*

*and furthermore this will be livestreamed to the monarch's many loyal fans with at least one camera pointed at the monarch's face and another pointed at the serf's torso and another pointed at the pile of manure*

The lawyers have greenlighted the legality with liberal interpretations of the words *monarch*, *serf* and *musket*.

He wants to start with the people who have personally insulted Him on social media.

As always, there are some of us for whom this is a red line. They tell him no, and they are gone.

For the time being, we have secretly hired lookalike stuntmen with blood packs, and replaced his favourite gun with an identical one that fires blanks.

On video, it actually all looks pretty cool.

***"You have been told so many lies…"***
**Tim Kiely**

she said, with a sad shake of her head
and the smile of one who expected resistance
to all the corrections that would now come.

In the halls of a dim museum, authoritative
in some sharp-shoulder suit, she told me
the history of 'Give Back The Vote Day',

showed me black-and-white photographs
of all who had marched to return their rights,
their placards inked with '*If It Ain't Broke*',

'*We Can't Be Trusted*' and '*I Know My Place*',
their faces grey and loud with
submission. Seeing me, her laugh

was a porcelain hand laid on my throat.
"*You were told democracy
was what the people wanted - it's not!*

*You talk about listening, but if you did
you would know how much they love to be governed
without their permission; how much trust they place*

*in the hands of those who promise only
to rock them back to an innocent sleep.
Really, I feel sorry for you…*"

I very nearly believed her, until
I saw the walls tremor. I remembered
her breaking into my head — knew how

I would wake up soon, and chase her
and her travesty of my history
                                      out.

# Beyond the Polished Table
## Maggie Veness
CW / TW: Sexual abuse

Rosa's thick plait traces her spine, its glossy black tip touching the waistband of her gathered skirt. She is not tall. Her breasts barely reach the tiled kitchen sink where she is scrubbing oven trays and saucepans, the raw cracks on her hands stinging in the soapy hot water.

 A movement outside draws her gaze through the window where the paper skin of a spent piñata flutters beneath the stark autumn light. From the high brick fence at the far end of the backyard a large terracotta sun-face smiles at her. Last night Mr Tony hosted a pool-party for his niece's thirteenth birthday. Mr Tony acts like a wealthy gringo. He went to work in America and returned after eight years with his pockets full of money. Burst balloons, paper cups and plates, streamers and candy wrappers litter the yard. A mess of ash and charcoal surrounds the fat-bellied chiminea. Rosa does not welcome the additional cleaning, but the extra money will mean she can buy fresh milk on the way home.

 A riot of coloured plastic furniture clutters the sprawling, wet pool-deck. The adobe brick home Rosa shares with her two young sons and her mother has three rooms but is still smaller than Mr Tony's pool. Before leaving today she must use the net to scoop out all the leaves and bugs. The turquoise, teal and silver pool tiles give the water's surface the same metallic sheen as the peacock feathers for sale in the market square. Dotted around the yard are six Giant Cohune and six Royal palms in brightly-patterned ceramic pots—egg yellow, orange, jungle green and sea blue. If Mr Tony notices the Cohune fronds are turning brown he will scratch his fingers into the dry soil and become angry, so today Rosa must also give extra water to each of the palms. She will certainly be late home.

 When polished leather shoes squeak across the flagstones behind her, she turns to see Mr Tony adjusting the starched collar of the white linen shirt she'd ironed yesterday. He clears his throat, filling the kitchen with cool authority.

 'Nice skirt,' he says, and plays his tongue over his front teeth.

 Rosa looks up into his bloodshot eyes. His face is bloated and his expression smug, like a dumb pig in a comic book. 'Gracias, Mr Tony,' she says, offering a modest smile. Her skirt is the same colour as his expensive electric toothbrush—the same toothbrush she uses each day to whisk away the streaks from his morning shit. She pats the course, mint-green fabric to dry her hands. 'You like Rosa make gorditas? Hot café?'

 Reaching to undo the button on his suit pants, he says, 'No. Lean over the table.'

 Her healthy young body is sometimes a blessing and sometimes a burden. Rosa polishes this table with vinegar and oil every day and the wood feels clean and smooth against her forehead. He likes to wind her plait loosely around her neck then clutch the coils with both hands. Limp with compliance as Mr Tony bucks and twitches between her splayed legs, once again she steers her thoughts toward arriving home—the joy she feels when her children run up and cling to her waist.

 She makes him a breakfast of scrambled eggs topped with chicken and Serrano peppers and brews strong, black coffee. He eats in silence, slowly flicking the pages of a thick document. She imagines some pages to be about José, her husband, who for the past year has been a model inmate in La Mesa Prison. José had stolen a milking cow to help fatten his children. His crime of simple theft carried a four-year sentence. That day she'd left the courthouse weeping, and stood at the bottom of the wide steps wondering how she could feed her family for the next four years. The store of butter and soft cheese she'd made had already run out. When Mr Tony approached with a handkerchief and an offer of paid work she sank to her knees with gratitude.

Today, José will once again appear before Mr Tony, this time applying to have his sentence reduced. Rosa expects leniency, confident that Mr Tony is pleased with her compliance and how well she cleans his hacienda. José could be home in just one year, or even less, a prospect that makes her eyes sting and her breath come fast.

Around noon Mr Tony summons his driver, then hands her an extra twenty-five pesos before departing for the courthouse. Enough for a bottle of milk. With so much cleaning to do before she can leave, and so far to walk, Rosa already knows she won't make it there in time to wave to her husband. She will have to wait until Mr Tony rises the following morning to learn the outcome of José's application.

She collects debris into a black garbage bag, but carries a smaller cotton bag for the barely touched cheese enchiladas, corn cobs on sticks and savory tamales. The wasted food is enough to feed her children, her mother and herself for two evenings, and supply her husband with an extra meal when she visits him on Saturday. As she forages and cleans, the midday sun burns her scalp. She trickles pool water over her canvas shoes to cool her feet. With the deck tidy, she scoops up a pile of damp towels, carries them to the laundry and loads the machine. Back outside, she takes the long-handled net and walks up and down the length of the pool until the water is clear. By now her hips and back ache. Unwinding the hose, she sets about watering the palms while dreaming of her bed—her children sleeping close beside her.

~

Trudging along the crushed gravel path at eight a.m., Rosa's heart beats fast and hard in anticipation of great news. She fills the next hours first by ironing and dusting, then by mopping the huge expanse of flagstone. It's almost eleven when Mr Tony finally enters the kitchen and announces that he has shortened José's sentence by six months. Bewildered, she clasps her hands to her chest. She has already given so much. How could it be worth so little? Helplessness and anger set her cheeks on fire.

'Muchísimas gracias Mr Tony.'

Rosa will not allow herself to crumble in his presence, but disappointment has soured her blood and her thoughts turn to acts of vengeance.

After Mr Tony takes his pleasure, he sits to read through a stack of papers and drink freshly brewed coffee while she prepares bacon frittata for his breakfast. As the chopped bacon sizzles, she slices an onion and two tomatoes and whisks four eggs. Rosa's mouth waters and her empty stomach contracts. Her family has not tasted bacon in a long time. She is lonely for José and her hands throb because they are never away from work long enough for the cracks to heal. Leaning forward over the egg mixture, she sends a curse down a string of spittle, then squares her shoulders and lifts her chin.

In a dream that night she sets a pack of wild dogs at Mr Tony's heels and watches as they bring him to the ground; listens as they crunch his bones. She wakes early with a clenched jaw, dismayed to find there were no wild dogs and he is still alive; miserable because his death is out of the question. She needs to keep this job for thirty more months. While Rosa can only dream about wild dogs, there are many ways to make him suffer.

She enters quietly through Mr Tony's back door. Rather than head straight to the sink she sits at the polished table with her thoughts. But recalling the crush of his weight quickly steals her breath, so she heads to the pantry to gather empty pickle jars.

By mid-afternoon she has trapped three of the same pale-yellow scorpions she regularly flattens and sweeps from the back patio. Before walking home she sets them free between his expensive bed-sheets. The scorpion's bite will cause Mr Tony terrible pain. He will phone for help and the nearby hospital will administer anti-venom. He will not die but he will feel very sick for many days. Too sick to take his pleasure.

As she walks, she whispers to her shadow, '¿Esta noche, dalor al diablo, no?' Tonight, pain for the devil, eh?

Soon, the rainy season will begin. By July, the trees and flowers will be in full bloom, attracting many insects and spiders. Rosa has seen the poisonous brown violin-shaped spiders in Mr Tony's garage, and her cousin Araceli was once bitten by a Black Widow and was very sick for two weeks. Rosa will make good use of the pickle jars.

Night will continue to follow day and then José will return to her and their young sons. He will once again find work in the corn and maize fields and she will leave this job. Her anger will burn itself out. Her hands will mend. And her husband will be the only one to lift her skirt.

**Right-hand page:**

**The Hand of a Writer**
Sarah-Jane Crowson

# JUST THE JOB  105

FIG. 17.—HAND OF A WRITER

weird fiction, distinguished by the under- sides of wings.
paradoxes, poetry, and fairy tales.
symbolism, sloe and bramble.
 oval imagination, bordered with silver

# Emptying Las Vegas
**Marie Papier**

Some do it with a spoon
as the saying has it
for emptying the ocean.

I did it with my eyes
closed   sipping a cappuccino
on a terrace in Bellagio

One by one
the big screens overhead
went blank
The Eiffel Tower lost its sheen
The Venetian Palace collapsed
into dust   Liberty sank
as darkness rose   as trash
shed its glitter

Beating drums dropped their rage
Metallic sounds their clunk
Motorbikes glided silently
as sailing boats on Colorado, as
condors over the big chasm
of Grand Canyon

           Then
I could hear the breathing
of the child asleep
at my side

# Gale
**Marie Papier**

Eccl. 1:6

*"The wind blows to the south*
*and to the north;*
*round and round it goes…"*
rips away the poem
she's writing on the terrace
of a small downtown café
about the fickleness of love

    *Brute*!
she shouts
            running after the page
the wind holds between its teeth
        hissing  taunting her
before letting go of the paper

            She stomps her foot on it
                loses her balance
when the wind   rushing back   lifts the poem
        chases it down the street
            on to the main square
flings it over the rooftops…


As good as published
        she thought.

# Intruders
## Desree

*Anguilla was first settled by Indigenous Amerindian peoples who migrated from South America. When Anguilla was first colonised by Europeans is uncertain: some sources claim that Columbus sighted the island during his second voyage in 1493, while others state that the first European explorer was the French Huguenot nobleman and merchant, René Goulaine de Laudonnière, in 1564.*

     In 1992, I arrived with a body too small to carry anything other than the smell of East-Enders. Returning each year, just like they had taught me in school, made it *mine*.

I wrapped my tongue around the accent hoping to abstract the coral and limestone, as though I were hollow. Telling stories of Mother to children she had never called inside for dinner.

                Oh, small island people, you have, again, welcomed visitors who plan to steal the shovel you grew them with. With hair as straight as rulers, they consumed everything offered to them, took everything that wasn't. Planted tobacco and sugar in your bloodline, claimed ignorance when the cancer spread.

                Oh, small island people. Do you not hear the settler in this accent? How I have come here to take what does not belong to me, name it ancestry? All I know of this land is what my grandmother taught me: we curtsy to the same Queen.

Malliouhana, they took your name, then baptised you eel, something slippery, mysterious, needing to be caught.
At least, I call you home.

# Oddjob
**Desree**

Here, when I'm in this office, I am Oddjob.
A squat, with arms like thighs, a sickly zoo-smell.
I do not have a razor-edged hat, or the ability to decide
when strangers can touch my hair. My words sit
eagerly in the roof of sink, next to the coffee machine.
Each time they feel ready for this new birth,
it proves to be another false labour.
Sarah reminds me that the words of Black Women
have a much longer gestation period. I can't work out
if I'm a mute or if I've been turned off at the wall.
Maybe this is just another forced sterilisation.

# Zarmina's baby
**Maria FitzGerald**

Her name is Zarmina.

She is world-weary —
Of the patrols that forbid her and other women
to enter Jerusalem without permits

World-weary —
Of the patrols that enforce body scans on her
and other women of the West Bank

World-weary —
Of the patrols that dismiss letters in Arabic
or Hebrew from doctors who know what will happen
… Zarmina waits and waits and she waits

Too late —

She delivers her first-born dead in an
unholy place: by an apartheid wall
where a soldier takes Zarmina's baby,
her child's corpse

Holds it aloft —
His prize.

Bone-weary, the women
cannot remember the words they spoke before pain
cannot look at a solider for fear of …
cannot look at their husbands for fear of …

know the griefs of their occupation
can never be undone

# They say I am the firstborn
**Martins Deep**

In Kaduna, we live in two rooms,
my parents and five

children outgrowing their skins,
they begin to widen the walls

each morning as they stretch. Four boys
and one girl numbering stars
on the ceiling

We live in two rooms,
and this means the only space left
is for passage and setting mouse traps

This means I could not be scared
of anything beneath the bed, after watching horror
movies at brother Kunle's — a neighbor

I could not be scared, because
under our bed is stuffed with too many things
to have space for monsters

Here, my father hid his house rent
anxieties and his creditors' threats

And mother — this is where she keeps
all her used balm containers she collects water into
the nights father invokes rain

The smiles on our faces in our family portrait
tell me even paradise has fossils. I stop
staring hard at it to not singe the photograph

and curiously bend to look under our bed
and find out father's house rent
anxiety is gone

In class, I unzip my schoolbag, wondering
why it is unusually heavy, today

I open it and find all of them
wrapped safely in a quit notice
within father's obituary.

# Catharsis
**Martins Deep**

It's 6:47 a.m. under an unwashed blanket; you're waking up to the wild
appetite of X, (an unknown value in the equation of grief) or,
you're only just curious about its feeding habit, habitat found
in your darkest scar.

You learn that this thing eats with its ears.
Also, that its favourite dish is the echo
of your voice
when it wails against what your eyes may never unsee.

It's freezing in here. I mean, the cave of your mouth,
where — when you pray — blackbirds flutter
to roost in the ears of your apartment walls,
like a sentence in your unsent letter
that finally rests; soaks sunlight on a marble headstone.

Your first prayer gets trapped by cobwebs
in the ears of God. Second prayer,
like a dart, misses a moth to shard the light bulb —

then replaced the hour hand to strike twelve
letting in that fever of longing smuggled through your nostrils
by the faint scent of an old friend, lover.

Here, you witness memory become
into water, to have your tongue
bring to remembrance your true poison
in front of the barmaid.

You watch it rise — this body of water,
first, drowning a man agonizing in Aramaic
on the wooden crucifix hanging down your neck
then your body. your broken body.

Saving grace can be experienced in several ways. Today, it is a gentle knock
on your door — a child's
brown eye through the peephole. A little girl
chewing dates to pronounce your name like a cantrip
vaporizing the troubled waters
into the white of your eyes.

# Genesis 1:3
**Joe Williams**

Like much of the Old Testament,
it's an over-simplification.
It's long enough as it is
without including explanations
of fundamental forces
or how incandescence occurs
when energy passes through a filament.

If only the ancient scholar
who transcribed these sacred lines
had asked for a bit more detail,
we could have saved a lot of time.

# Part Time Anarchist
## Joe Williams

I'm a part time anarchist. I want to smash the system.
I once threw an egg at Boris Johnson, but I missed him.
In hindsight it was probably a bad idea to fry it,
but I don't care for details, I just want to riot.

I'm a part time anarchist. Down with the state!
Conformity, complicity, that's what I hate.
On my bedroom wall I've got a Che Guevara poster,
and when I have a cup of tea I never use a coaster.

I'm a part time anarchist. Screw your stupid rules!
I run and duck and divebomb when I'm at the swimming pool.
I go into the library to have a conversation.
I always flush the toilet when the train is in the station.

I'm a part time anarchist, only at weekends.
When Monday morning comes around I'm back at work again.
I've got a job with Daddy's firm. He's a merchant banker.
I'm a part time anarchist, full time wanker.

# The Politician
## Bill Lythgoe

He stands up, speaks up for what he believes in,
makes the words and sentences fit
the ideas he knows are so important
and need to be stated in eloquent style
as simple, basic common sense
with no ambiguous turn of phrase
that could be taken out of context
by a scheming opposition.

He reels off carefully chosen statistics
to prove to us that what he proposes
is obvious to all and sundry
and not just something based upon
a soundbite stretched into a sound,
election-winning manifesto
resulting in a mandate from
a quarter of the population.

He needs to make it crystal clear
he's on the side of hard-working families
and wants to build affordable homes
and make our borders more secure.
He says he'll do whatever it takes
to welcome people from abroad
who share our values and our wish
to make our borders more secure.

He's never been influenced by ambition
or the millions donated by loyal supporters
rewarded by seats in the House of Lords,
or the billionaires who own the free press,
or old school chums with top jobs in the City
whose tax returns are completely transparent
and guaranteed by PricewaterhouseCoopers
to contain no traces of any wrongdoing.

He sits down to polite applause.
His speechwriter rests a hand on his shoulder
and reassures him that next time out –
in front of the press and the TV cameras –
with a little more practice, he'll make the grade.

# Secrets of a cartographer's wife
**Katrina Dybzynska**

The cartographer's wife never told him
about her contributions to the maps.
Few tiny islands hidden in the middle
of an archipelago in the name of symmetry.
Some border line moved to more resemble
a face shape. The territory of England shortened
slightly, in a personal revenge.

One time, she renamed an insignificant river
in Bangladesh, after her lover. She pitied
the cartographer for being more furious
about the affair than about her intervention
in the world order. She knew that romances
were ephemeral, while naming things
changed them forever.

# The Dictator's Wife watching ships
**Katrina Dybzynska**

My husband thinks the sea should be reserved
for navy fleet, cargo vessels and luxurious yachts.
He can't stand unpredictability and the patience
of sailboats. He enjoys the flags and is comfortable
with the liners that navigate from A to B,

yet free-flowing horizon has no place is his calculations.
At least till the next war, when the prospect of conquering
will wake up the explorer in him. He analyses the curve
of losses and gains though he does not call them losses.
Maybe underperforming currents.

He does not hear the storm coming, even if he always fears
the sudden change of luck. He would never claim luck,
he plans for the weather. He prefers the reliable structure
of a harbor to the dirt of a beach. He never observes the waves.
That is how I know he will be overthrown.

I like watching the ships disappear. It's so easy
for them to glide out of the picture.

# [superpower vs sinopower]
## Yuan Changming

You cut meat with sharp knives
        We poke grasses with bamboo sticks

        You punch others with hard fists
We dance around you with *taichi* gestures

        Your men fuck around everywhere outside your households
Our women lay babies right in your living rooms

        You colonize every city with an English syntax
We decorate each street with Chinese signboards

        You deploy aircraft carriers near our waters and coasts
We marry girls to your princes and paupers

You enjoy setting fires and blowing winds along our long walls
        We have Chinese stomachs to digest all insults and injuries

You try every way to overthrow our government
        We sell every artifact to help your people survive

        You borrow money from us to build more weapons
We work hard to make more money for your banks

# [the greatest soft power: for qi hong]
## Yuan Changming

What softens
                        A human heart is
Neither money nor honey

Rather, it is a good natured smile of
Some dog playing with a cat, a bird
Feeding her young with her broken wings
Covering them against cold rain at noon
The whispering of a zephyr blowing
From nowhere, the mist flirting fitfully
With the copse at twilight, the flower
Trying to outlive its destiny, as well

As the few words you actually meant
To say to her but somehow you forgot
                    In the tender of last night

## doubt is our product
**Nick Allen**

*(A found poem; all text taken from the article* Truth Decay *by Michiko Kakutani; The Guardian 14 July 2018)*

diminish the value of truth – fake news and alternative facts – dezinformatsiya - *Everyone is entitled to his own opinion, but not to his own facts*\*

the Rashomon effect - all truths are partial - the gospel of postmodernism - there are no universal truths   only smaller personal truths - all truths are partial - relativistic arguments have been hijacked - a wilful hostility to established knowledge - all truths are partial - teach intelligent design alongside evolution   teach the controversy - ignorance is strength

the tobacco strategy - doubt is our product - avoid transparency   define reality on your own terms - confuse balance with truth-telling   wilful neutrality with accuracy - all truths are partial - the conditions that make a people susceptible to political manipulation - watch the news on mute - all truths are partial - wake up the sheeple - assert power over truth

*the sheer fact of self   the only real thing in an unreal environment*\*\* - relativism synched with narcissism - present both sides - all truths are partial - replace expertise with the wisdom of the crowd - ironic Nazi iconography - the internet doesn't just reflect reality - watch the news on mute - the internet doesn't just reflect reality anymore   it shapes it

*political chaos is connected with the decay of language*\*\*\* - the chasm between the leaders real and declared aims - accusing people of the very sins the accuser is guilty of - translate grammatical anarchy - stop inviting cranks on to science programmes - be truthful   not neutral

without commonly agreed facts   no rational debate   no substantive means of evaluating candidates   no way to hold elected officials accountable - without truth democracy is hobbled - ignorance is strength

all truths are partial - watch the news on mute - doubt is our product


(\*Patrick Moynihan; \*\*Philip Roth; \*\*\*George Orwell)

# Community Service
**Carter Lappin**

When the man who runs the corner store on our block catches a boy from our neighbourhood stealing, he calls in my grandmother instead of the police. The police don't come to this neighbourhood, not if they don't have to.

Grandmother slings her shawl over her shoulders and marches all five-foot nothing of herself down there to grab the boy by the ear. When she scolds him, she uses his full name, middle and last included. She was there when he was born, as she was when most of us around here were. She makes him apologize, sheepish, to the shopkeeper, before dragging the boy from the store.

The shopkeeper waves goodbye. Next time she goes shopping, Grandmother will find an extra orange slipped into the bottom of her cloth grocery bag.

She's spoken to this boy two, maybe three times in his life. Within a day, I find him up to his knees in soil, tending to my grandmother's rooftop garden with a look of contrition on his face. Grandmother is supervising from nearby, sipping lemonade from her favourite glass and warning him not to break any of the tender stalks of green if he can help it.

He grumbles, but he's extra-careful after that.

I sit next to Grandmother, then, and together we watch things grow.

# The Bees
## Julie Stevens

A noise so fierce it shook us.
Heads turned and saw the ground rising,
a swarm of blades in a blanket to smother.

We couldn't see their hidden knives
but knew they carried harm,
would puncture our tongues.

Their orchestra of violent strings
surged together, throwing fear
to this chair that dragged me down.

Would they know I couldn't leave?
Would they drape themselves over
and heave me away?

This black shadow was an advancing mob
buzzing death into every note
and here I was, fixed underneath.

No muscle to rise and flee,
no legs to run faster
than their fearsome flight.

As my world caved in,
I was forced to race
with the power of still.

**Woman**
Charlotte Jung

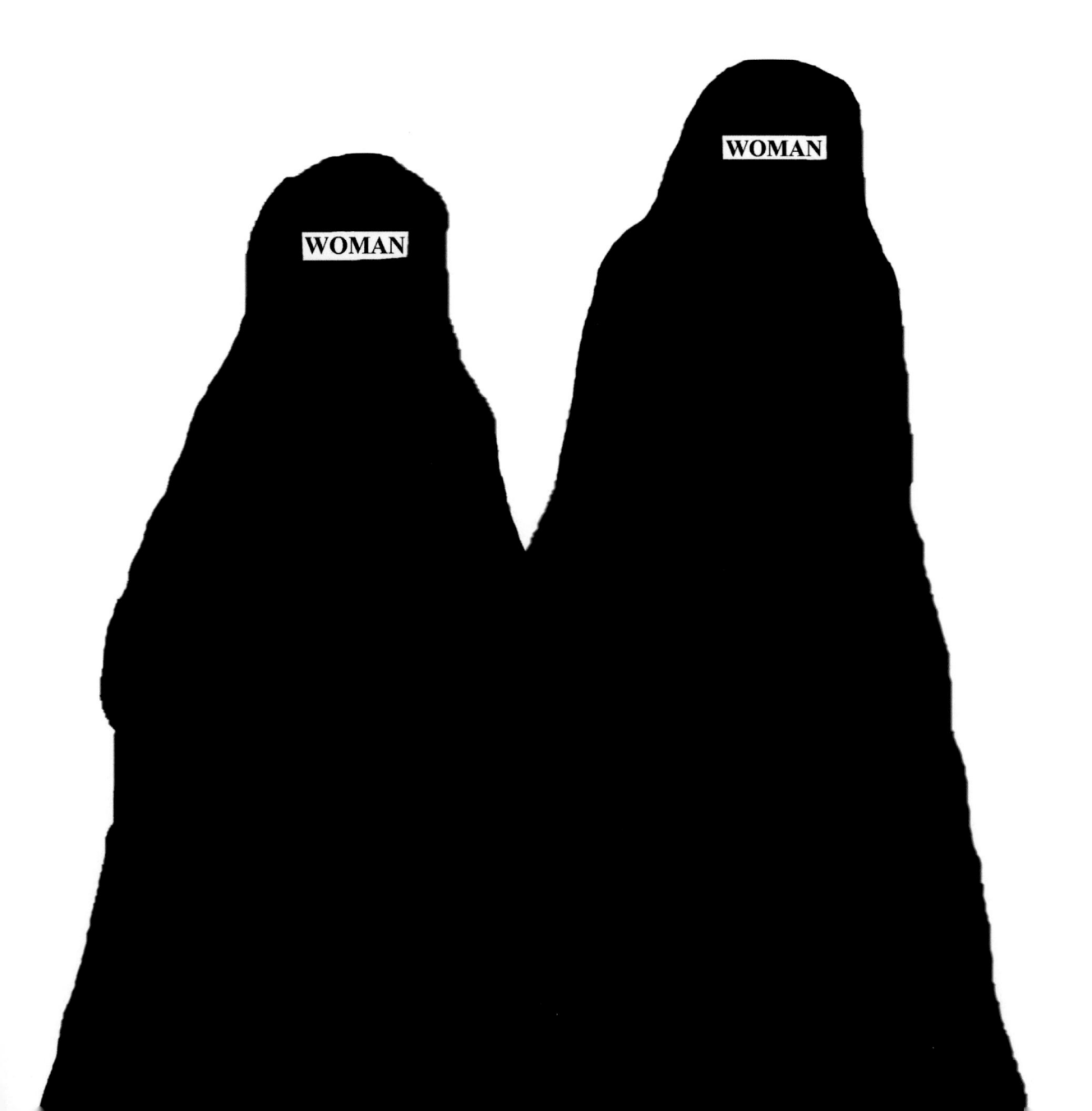

# You Can't Always Get the Stains Out
## Jennifer Rowe

Pa leans back against the plastic table I'm sitting under; it scrapes back against my foot and I freeze. It's dark outside, and across the street, I can see our neon 'Laundromat' sign reflected in Miss Simpkin's window.

"I hear you need my help, Mr Drayton?"

Another scrape, and I shuffle back some. I really don't wanna be found out. I sit quiet under the table cos I like to draw customers. Big and tall, short and thin, old ladies swaddled in blankets, kids dragging more laundry than they can carry. Most wanna talk to Pa cos he's good at listening and even better at helping. Then there's people like Mr NavyPants.

"I hear you're good at... cleaning things up?"

Mr NavyPants has orange socks; I can see a label that says Beeching. It's a highfalutin' name for socks so he must be rich – either that or he's got rich sock-buying friends.

Pa laughs. "There's no need for innuendo here."

I draw NavyPants' face, it's easy cos he's not got much showing below his hat and above his scarf, just a very sharp triangular nose.

"It's just you, me and the right price," says Pa.

The table scrapes again; I hold my breath and count to five.

I've been drawing all my life, so Pa says. My last birthday, he bought me a whole new box of colouring pens. It was the biggest present I ever got and I think it was cos Mom went away. I got a lot of new things since then, but Mom always gave me crayons, so that's what I use. Don't need fancy stuff to draw.

"Here," Mr NavyPants says. There's a rustling. "This is Davina."

"Uh-huh." Pa's feet walk away toward the floor lamp until I can see all of him. He holds up a photo to the light and whistles.

"I love her but she's terrible trouble." He shifts from one navy leg to the other. "My wife... you know."

"Ah." Pa peers outside. "No 'friends' with you today?"

Navypants doesn't move. "Just you and me."

Pa smiles and pockets the picture. "Good."

"You can clean it all up by next week?" NavyPants edges toward the exit. "Only, the elections...".

"Just wire me the money."

Pa watches him leave, then heads to his office and closes the door.

I finish off drawing Mr NavyPants. With his face half-covered, he looks like a gangster, so I give him shoes with spikes on the heel and a black briefcase.

The door jangles as a boy drags in a huge bag of washing. It's Jake, the courier.

"Laundry!" he shouts. Then, seeing no-one's about, he takes a complimentary mint from the 'customers only' candy jar, and leaves.

I unfold myself from under the table and go knock on the office door. "Pa!"

Everyone tells me I'm good at drawing. But Pa says "don't get above yourself. Not everyone's gonna tell you what you wanna hear." Mrs Aloupis, though, next door, she always sees the likenesses, and *her* paintings are in galleries.

I hear Pa, muffled, on the telephone. "Nominee Drayton wants his affair cleaned up. You available?"

I knock.

"Well, I reckon he's the best chance we have, don't you?"

"Pa?"

"Just pay her off – and create a diversion, in case anyone gets wind."

"Pa!"

"A diversion. A div… Just make the lady an offer she can't refuse and get the press off Drayton, willya?"

I'm just wondering "who's got wind?" when Pa opens the door.

"Hey Humbug!" He looks at the bundle of clothes. "Gonna help me load the machine?"

"I sure am, Pa. I like cleaning stuff."

"Me too," he says, "me too."

Next day, breakfast TV says the History Museum's burning. Pa shakes his head and mumbles, "Too much, too much."

Later, Mr NavyPants appears on the screen and he's giving a speech about how families should stay together in "these difficult times." I think of Mom and wonder where she is.

All my pictures of the laundromat people are hidden in my room, cos Pa doesn't know I sit under the table. He wants me upstairs learning spelling or out playing, but I like the smell of the soap and the 'shuh-shuh' of the machines turning. Besides, Pa says outside's not so safe these days.

"But things are changing, Jenna, just you see." He squeezes my arm and smiles. "Soon as we get a new guy in charge, huh?"

We don't see Mr NavyPants again, least not in the Laundromat. Months later, though, Mr BlackBoots walks in and locks the door behind him. He and Pa talk about 'Mr President,' but I already know they mean Navypants cos I've seen him on the TV.

"He's got a clean-up job for you," he tells Pa, and talks about a lot of money that's got accidentally spent. When he's gone Pa kicks the wastebasket. I draw BlackBoots with wings made of dollar signs and hang it in my room.

Later that week, there is an explosion in the city and Pa says it was a bank vault where they keep gold – only the gold's not there anymore. Some people died, he says, and that's bad.

That afternoon, Pa stands in front of the dryer for a real long time.

More people start to come into the laundromat each day. Most of them sad or angry or both; Pa tries to help, I think. I want to draw them but they pace about a lot. Pa says people don't trust President Drayton anymore. I start to tell him I'm not surprised with those socks, but then I remember I've never seen them before.

We don't see Mr BlackBoots again until after my next birthday. I'm still wearing my 'I am 9' button when he visits. The power's gone off again, so Pa switches on the generator and turns on a hot wash.

"There's a problem." Mr Boots wipes his hands on his Grey Slacks. "This one's big."

The washing machine goes shuh-shuh as it turns and I can't hear everything they say. Pa told me once that when a washing machine drum turns full circle, it's called a revolution. I draw Pa and President Drayton and BlackBoots all revolutionising together inside the big washer; spinning round and round.

When I've been nine for nearly three months, a thing called a Civil War starts. Pa says "don't worry, Humbug," but there're people shouting outside and someone broke our window so it's half taped-up. I wonder if Mom's okay, wherever she is. I draw her and me and Pa in a house in the countryside; it's just us and we have big smiles.

We watch Mr NavyPants – now Mr MilitaryUniform – on the TV, telling everyone to "calm down." There are lots of men who look like him and they're all carrying guns. BlackBoots is there too – always close by. I hear "for your own safety…" and "…shot on sight…" That night, as I'm wondering what a curfew is, we hear gunshots nearby and somebody screams. Pa locks the laundromat door and flips the sign over.

"We closing up, Pa?"

"Go get your coat, Humbug."

"Where we going?"

"I'll tell you when we get there, but go get your coat."

When I come back, he's been in my room and packed a bag. All my drawings are in the waste-bin and his eyes are wet.

"Pa? I'm sorry, Pa."

"It's OK, Humbug. I'm sorry too." He flicks a match into the bin and we watch them curl up and burn. When it's done, there's a few little pieces left.

"Pa? What about the machines? We taking them too?"

He walks toward the window and looks out. "There's nothing gonna get this lot clean, Pickle." He turns back to me, shrugs and heads out back. "Ready to go in five, okay?"

There are a few charred pieces left in the bin. I try to match them up: a sharp nose, Mom smiling, dollar signs. I screw them up and push them to the bottom.

Out across the street, I can still see Pa's sign, reflected in Miss Simpkins' window:

'Dirty Laundry – no job too big'.

# Fish
**Eve Chancellor**

When I was twelve,
my father taught me
how to catch a fish:
a shimmering, silver
bream
       the exact length
of his
     handspan.

Carefully, with gentle
fingers,
he slipped the fish
off the tackle
and handed it
to me.
A gift.

The creature lay there,
in the palm of my hand,
breathing on one side,
gasping and grasping
for life;
drowning on air,
its body wretched
and trembling
in shuddering
paroxysms
of fear.

I felt it then:
the power
in my hands;
the strength
of my fingers
to take another life,
so weak and fragile.

*We put it back*,
my father taught me.

*That's why we always*
put them back.

# The Date
## Kevin Crowe

When the waitress poured a small amount of wine in his glass, he swirled the liquid, placed it under his nose, took a sniff and then a taste. He put the glass down and said to her: "The wine's corked. It needs replacing."

Ignoring the waitress as she took the bottle away, he turned to the woman sitting opposite and said: "Just look at her! Dyed black hair, purple lips, a ring in her nose that makes her look like she's dripping snot and a face plastered with so much white slap it'd probably crack if she smiled. Shouldn't be allowed in a place like this."

The woman said: "I didn't know screw-top wine could be corked." This brought a quick smile from the waitress who was at that moment depositing the replacement bottle on the table.

The man explained in great detail what being corked meant and what caused it. In such detail that she had finished her starter before he had even begun his. When the waitress asked if they were ready for the main course, he pointed to his starter and said: "Does it look like it?" Then waving his hand at his still-full plate, said: "Take it away. It's inedible anyway. I won't be paying for it."

He smiled at his date. "I've had better service at McDonald's – and more edible food." He took a swig of his wine, then said: "It was great meeting you again after all these years. Though how you can stand living in this godforsaken place, what with the rain and wind and midges, I don't know. A week is long enough for me."

She began to answer, but she spoke no more than half a dozen words before he interrupted, changing the subject and talking about politics, music, literature, sport, work and himself. Mainly himself. Occasionally he asked her a question, but never allowed her the time to answer.

She drank her share of the wine and ate, nodding or shaking her head as appropriate, rarely bothering with eye contact. At least not with him. He continued his criticism of the waitress, referring to her as looking like a zombie, saying, "I feel like an extra in a Walking Dead film."

His date's smile didn't reach her eyes.

After paying the bill, he leaned forward and, a leer on his face, asked: "Do you fancy coming back to my hotel for a nightcap? Get to renew our acquaintance in more depth?"

She shook her head as she stood up. "It's been an instructive evening. Thanks, but no I won't be going for a nightcap. I have to see my daughter gets home safely now she's finished her shift."

The waitress had already put on her coat and the two women walked out of the restaurant together.

# Rubble (The Demolished People)
**Thomas Lawrance**

The explosive charges were placed carefully around his slippered feet. The grandchildren said their final goodbyes — though it had been explained to them that he didn't recognise their faces anymore — and then stepped back with the guiding hands of parents on their shoulders. A line of safety tape was drawn across the living room.

A number of the gathered focused their phones, and the countdown commenced. A beat after 'one', the charges went off, and the old man fell stiffly into his own footprint. In his place, a pillar of dust dissipated to applause. The family moved chattering into the garden — dad pausing to check that there were no scratches on the fireplace (and then, satisfied, heading out to light the barbecue) — and the man from the council moved in with his dustpan and binbag. He weighed the rubble of the demolished man, and set off for the next address on his list.


The Minister jabbed at the air with a slanted fist, thumb pressed down over his index finger, as if scraping stubborn dirt from a surface with his thumbnail. He was reaffirming the benefits of his scheme.

"… a small controlled explosion. We take the resultant rubble, and we use it to fill the potholes in our roads. To repair bridges. To build good, strong spaces for our businesses. To save money for your healthcare. To provide for the hard-working people of this country."

The subjects of the Minister's demolition scheme were the senile, the infirm, the unwelcome, the unfit for work, the unable to vote. At first, individuals were donated for demolition by their families and friends, who were promised generous payments for their contribution, but by now the council just seemed to know who was next. They had lists.

"Per demolishee, we recover one hundred and fifty pounds of useful material. In the rubble of a demolished life," the Minister smiled warmly, "we find thirty bricks of the future."


In night's shadows, behind a chain-link fence, three children watched a homeless man in some distress. Two men from the council were trying to restrain him, and from a van, pulling up with a screech, jumped a third. In their hi-vis triangulation, they surrounded the homeless man under the darkened archway of a railway bridge. The children vied for positions of optimal observation as the three captors bound the homeless man with wire, before setting charges at his feet. They checked his pockets and snapped a watch from his wrist (shaken, held up to a councilman's ear, and tossed aside). The three captors took their regulatory paces back. As a train came thundering overhead, a swift succession of flashes illuminated the underside of the bridge, parting the stagnant waters of puddles and blowing away leaves.

The rubble of the homeless man was duly bagged and weighed and thrown into the back of the van. Cycling away on their streetlit route home, the children agreed that there was there was nothing left to see.

## Passing a statue of a lion hunting a gazelle in Victoria
**Christian Ward**

For a moment, the gazelle pins the lion
down. Hooves, bright as polished obsidian,
pressed on its throat. Horns, twisted
as a spiral staircase, poised to smash
through its helpless skull. A scene dramatic
enough to make Attenborough wince.
Should the gazelle go through with it,
think of the consequences. Every animal
on the savannah a pawn in a greater game.
The gazelle cannot smile. But, in the moment
when the lion is reduced to play dough,
the gazelle understands how fear sidling
across your chest like a snake is greater
than a mouthful of teeth poised for the kill.
For a moment, I blinked into a gazelle.
Watched you wince as I walked away,
the setting sun bloody and shrinking like your heart.

**Left and right-hand side: Untitled**
Despy Boutris

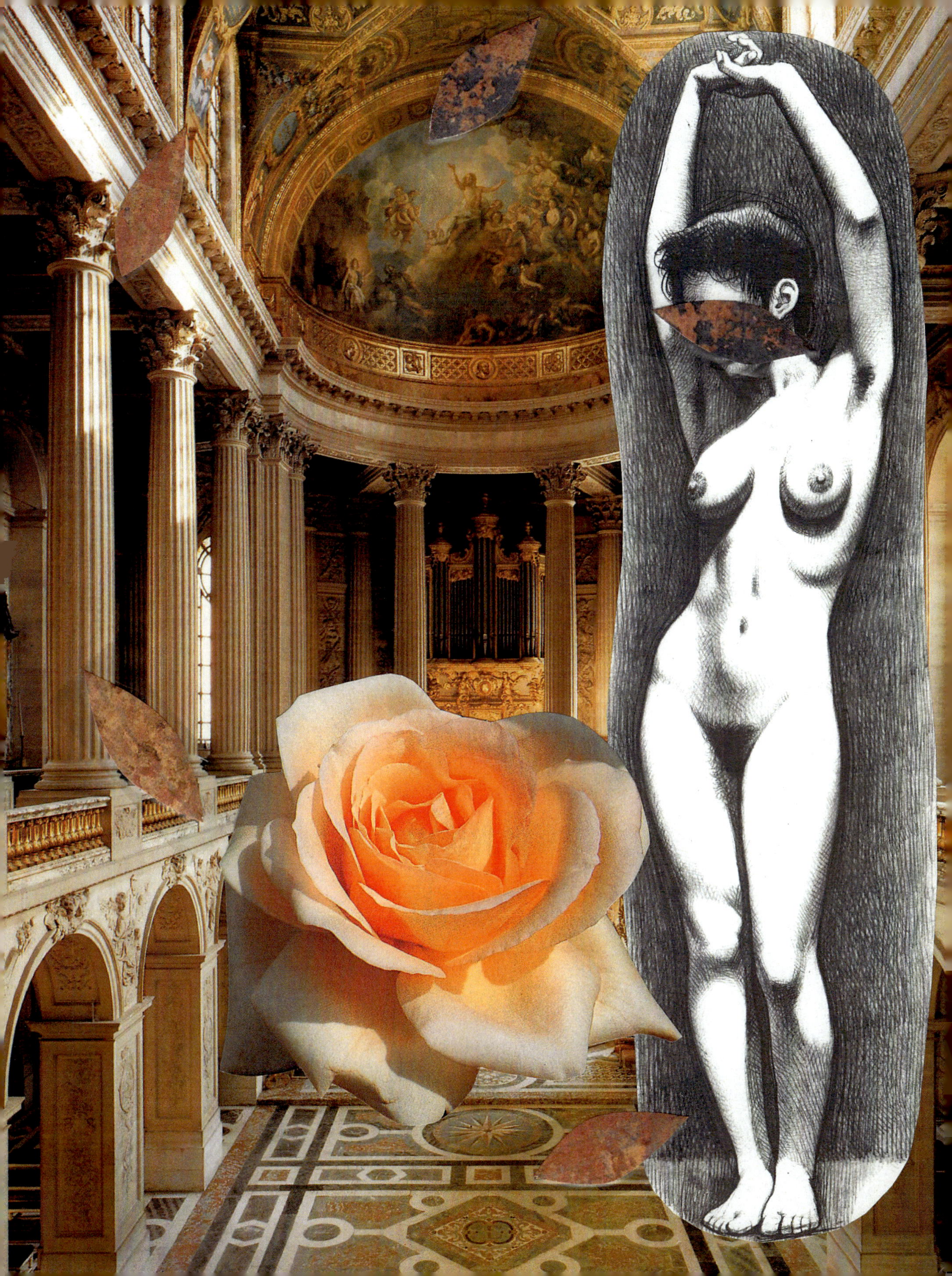

## Review of 'Things I Have Forgotten Before' by Tanatsei Gambura, published by Bad Betty Press
## Tim Kiely

I was editing a pamphlet recently. I had just finished reading it aloud to my fiancée, and I asked her, "*did you find anything was missing?*" She remarked that it was an odd question, and pointed out that she might have some difficulty in answering if she didn't know from the outset that she was meant to be looking for it. Being conscious of an absence, being aware of something that isn't there, might be the closest, philosophically speaking, that an atheist and materialist can ever come to something like a religious belief. Certainly, as the great religions have always known, the language of omission and negation offers a way to address the inexpressible. But such language also often assumes a much more sinister aspect, especially in a political reality beset by more malign erasures.

Tanatsei Gambura deploys this notion of erasure especially deftly. Setting her pamphlet partially in the political context of modern Zimbabwe, where an oppressive government apparatus means that whole zones of discussion must simply be avoided for safety's sake, her omissions and self-censorship work explicitly to foreground those uncomfortable realities which are *not* being discussed.

The poem 'Cause of Death' imagines the enforced quiet of a dinner party where the subject of political disappearances is not broached because "*[w]e do not / discuss politics / at the dining table*," but the very fact of such enforced silence means that the thing being avoided is never far from the attention of those assembled, even as they "*stab… with a fork… lift… to a trembling / mouth and swallow.*" For all of the community's insistence on silence, the mechanisms of political repression are not subtle.

The title poem deals with the idea of things which have been deliberately 'forgotten' as a means of processing trauma, but which nevertheless hover on the edge of recovery and disclosure. The process of moving from Harare to Johannesburg, and thereafter to an airport in Ethiopia and to an "*otherplace*" of unknown coordinates, prompts the persona to begin a process of deliberate vanishing, crouching against the walls "*like a dewy fungus,*" hiding in the familiar smells of their own clothes and dreaming of eventual disappearance. These are things which, the poem suggests, even as they have been 'forgotten', must be remembered.

Gambura's poetry is a corrective against the complacent assumptions of those societies in the Global North where Gambura now lives and works, with their own omissions and erasures of bodies of colour from the Global South. 'Photograph of a Black Girl on a Straße in Bonn' invites the reader to scan from the bottom upwards, noting a black girl in the foreground, but then taking in the "*ring of white faces,*" the "*thirty small windows*" observing her as the most dominant reality of both the picture and the poem itself, a black body buried under the constant scrutiny of observation (including by the reader).

The South African novelist J.M. Coetzee has spoken of the body, and the suffering visited upon it, as something that speaks with an irresistible authority, flummoxing all attempts to deny or trivialise it. As he puts it in 'Doubling the Point': "*it is not that one grants the authority of the suffering body: the suffering body takes this authority… its power is undeniable.*"

Gambura also works to foreground the body and its obstinate reality, as the thing which both evades final definition and which then demands its encounter with the reader. The theological spectre of the *via negativa* is raised, briefly, in the poem 'Planning a Naming Ceremony for Things We Do Not Know How to Name,' but exists alongside the unspeakable (in more ways than one) reality of the suffering of black bodies through colonialism – bodies that are "*the only archive of truth*" and whose violated presence (and absence) are a vivid haunting. In visions of ships falling to the bottom of the ocean, and black rivers which do not meet the sea, we are offered the horrifying distortion of an intangible "freedom" in silence and non-existence: "*If it is God, consider he's asleep… the apocalypse has already happened.*"

'Diagram of a Phone Screen Belonging to the SAPS Officer Processing My Documents' deals explicitly with such power structures as they appear in a contemporary South African context. The poem imagines the "*other girls… trapped in that screen*" as the "*big*" South African policeman toys with offering the persona the clearance documents she needs, for an implied price. As much as this poem seems to reinforce the dramatic disempowerment of the "*small, Zimbabwean, girl*" who narrates it, the fact that it ends with her "*discretion*", choosing between the social media hashtags that can both confirm her solidarity with other victims ("*#AmINext*") and call out the racism that still plagues South African society ("*#PutSouthAfricansFirst*") strikes me as just such an example of the suffering body "*taking*" its authority as the poem ends. Racists and bigots of all stripes know this power of calling attention to injustice – it is why their implied response to being made aware of it, embodied in that second hashtag, can only be defensive rage.

Popular critics of contemporary poetry, including where it intersects with spoken word, sometimes speak as if its practitioners were all loud, upfront, heart-on-sleeve discursiveness, with no appreciation for, or ability to deploy, the implied and the unstated. Gambura's pamphlet presents one very powerful counter-argument, and in so doing lays bare the sullen, thwarted resentment of those who would like to see less of her and her poetics. You may be sure that both Gambura and other artists of colour will still be there, even when their presence is not always obvious.

# Biographies

1. Alex Reed is a poet living in Northumberland. His previous pamphlets *A Career in Accompaniment* and *These Nights at Home* explore themes of illness, care-giving and loss. His first full collection, *knots, tangles, fankles* (V.Press, 2021) is a poetic response to R.D. Laing & A. Esterson's classic sixties text *Sanity, Madness & the Family*.
2. Bill Lythgoe is a retired primary school teacher and has been writing poetry seriously for about ten years. He has won prizes awarded by Writing Magazine, Sentinel Literary Quarterly, Fire River Poets, the Wakefield Red Shed, Creative Writing Ink and Nottingham Poetry Society, and been published by Earlyworks Press, Strong Verse, Southport Fringe Poetry and Gordon Square Review(Cleveland Ohio). If you Google *Bill Lythgoe poems* you can read some of his work.
3. Bonnie Meekums: Bonnie's 2020 novel, *A Kind of Family*, was published by Between the Lines. Her joint working-class childhood memoir with sister Jackie Hales, *Remnants of War*, was self-published in 2021. Other words appear in Dear Damsels, Reflex Press, Moss Puppy, Open Page and the Poetry Health Service, among other liminal and paper locations. Bonnie lives with her husband in Greater Manchester where she grows disobedient vegetables, hill walks, reads, dances, and from which she travels alarming distances to visit people she loves who have inconveniently chosen to live as far away from her as possible. Twitter: @bonniemeekums
4. Carter Lappin is an author from California. She has a bachelor's degree in creative writing and is scheduled to appear in a number of upcoming literary publications, including Falling Star Magazine.
5. Charlotte Jung is a visual poet, originally from Stockholm, Sweden and today she divides her time between the Stockholm countryside, and her adopted hometown Chicago. Chapbooks published; *MBRYO* (Puddles of Sky Press, 2019), *(SEED)* (Timglaset Editions, 2020), *HOLE BEING* (NoPress, 2021) and *ABCDE* (Trombone, 2021). Please see www.charlottejungwriter.com for more information about Charlotte and her writing.
6. Christian Ward is a UK based writer who can be currently found in *Wild Greens* and *Cold Moon Review*. Future poems will be appearing in *Uppagus*, *Chantarelle's Notebook* and *Spillwords*.
7. Despy Boutris's writing has been published or is forthcoming in American Poetry Review, American Literary Review, Copper Nickel, The Journal, Colorado Review, Prairie Schooner, and elsewhere. She teaches at the University of Houston, works as Assistant Poetry Editor for Gulf Coast, and serves as Editor-in-Chief of The West Review.
8. Desree is an award-winning spoken word artist, writer, playwright and facilitator based in London and Slough. Producer for both *Word Up* and *Word Of Mouth*, and TEDx speaker, she has featured at events around the UK and internationally. Desree has a pamphlet, *I Find My Strength In Simple Things (Burning Eye)*.
9. Eunice Ukamaka is a Nigerian self taught artist, whose work is forthcoming in the Epoch

Press's Third Issue. Eunice, who also majors in English and Literature in the university is a firm believer of "Life imitates Art, more than Art itself". She sees the world through a pencil and a paint brush and hopes to show everyday reality through her art.
10. Eve Chancellor is a Teacher of English in Manchester, and she has previously studied in Liverpool and Melbourne. She has an MLitt in Victorian Literature from the University of Glasgow, with a specialism in the role of childhood in 19th Century fiction. She is a member of SCBWI, graduate of the Golden Egg Academy and published on East of the Web.
11. Jenny Rowe is an actor and improviser, living in Sussex, UK, with her husband. She enjoys hiking the South Downs and being obsessed with other people's dogs until she can get one of her own.
12. UK based neurodivergent writer Jane Ayres completed a Creative Writing MA at the University of Kent in 2019 aged 57. She is fascinated by hybrid poetry/prose experimental forms and has work in *Dissonance, Lighthouse, Streetcake, The North, The Poetry Village, Door is a Jar, Kissing Dynamite, (mac)ro(mic), Selcouth Station, Crow of Minerva, Ample Remains, Sledgehammer* and *The Forge*. In 2020, she was longlisted for the Rebecca Swift Foundation Women Poets' Prize and her work has been nominated for the 2021 Best of the Net.
13. Joe Williams is a writer and performing poet from Leeds. His latest book is 'The Taking Part', a short collection of poems on the theme of sport and games, published by Maytree Press. His verse novella 'An Otley Run', was shortlisted for Best Novella at the 2019 Saboteur Awards. www.joewilliams.co.uk
14. John Winder is a landscape photographer working mainly in the medium of black and white. He began creative photography 40 years ago and is still surprised by the pleasure of both the act of photography and the resulting images. He enjoys the outdoors, nature and the environment.
15. Julie Stevens writes poems sometimes reflecting the impact Multiple Sclerosis (MS) has on her life. Her poems have recently been published on Ink Sweat & Tears, Sarasvati, and The Honest Ulsterman. Her winning Stickleback pamphlet *Balancing Act* was published by Hedgehog Poetry Press (June 2021) and her debut chapbook *Quicksand* by Dreich (Sept 2020). Website: www.jumpingjulespoetry.com. Twitter @julesjumping
16. Kate Young's poetry has appeared in various webzines and it has also featured in the anthologies Places of Poetry and Write Out Loud. Her pamphlet A Spark in the Darkness is due to be published with Hedgehog Press. Find her on Twitter @Kateyoung12poet.
17. Katrina Dybzynska is an internationally awarded writer published in Ireland, the UK, the US, Australia, Germany, and Poland. Currently, she is working on a book that explores power, resistance, and compliance dynamics. Polish Non-Fiction Institute graduate and BA-MA Researcher for Global Center for Advanced Studies. Her main focus is climate justice, migration, and overpopulation. She is passionate about the narratives of uncivilization, indigenous cosmologies, and decolonization.
18. Kevin Crowe lives in the Scottish Highlands with his husband Simon. He is the author of the short story collection "No Home In This World" (Fly-On-The-Wall Press, 2020); editor of the Highlands LGBT+ magazine "UnDividingLines"; has been published in many magazines,

anthologies and ezines and read online and at literary festivals.

19. Maggie Veness writes from Australia, where she has a view of the water to help keep her calm. Her credits include SLICE, Gem Street, LITRO, Award Winning Australian Writing, Page 17, Paris Lit Up, NAZAR, Bare Fiction, ADANNA, Best Lesbian Erotica, Bravado, Vine Leaves Literary Journal, plus scores of other fine literary journals, magazines, and anthologies across 10 countries to date. She enjoys music, red wine, long beach walks and feels lucky to be Australian.

20. Maria FitzGerald writes about identity, motherhood, love, loss and our interactions with Nature and place. She is a recipient of a Poetry Ireland New Poet Bursary (2021/2022). Further work is forthcoming in The Stinging Fly and Dedalus Press, Local Wonders anthology.

21. Marie Papier: A London Poetry School Student for the last 8 years, Marie has attended master classes, Seminars with Philip Gross and Greta Stoddart. Her poems are published by Arvon/Daily Telegraph, The North, Agenda, Stand, The Lighthouse, London Southbank Poetry, smith/doorstop anthology Poems about Running; Online; in Calyx, and Weather Indoors, two anthologies from Bristol Stanza (a member).

22. Martins Deep (he/him) is an Urhobo poet living in Kaduna, Nigeria. He is a photographer, digital artist, & currently a student of Ahmadu Bello University, Zaria. His most recent works have appeared, or are forthcoming, in Lolwe, 20.35 Africa: An Anthology of Contemporary Poetry, FIYAH, Cutbank Literary Journal, Blackbird Review, Brittle Paper, Barren Magazine, Agbowó Magazine, & elsewhere. He tweets @martinsdeep1

23. Michael Conley is a prose writer and poet from Manchester, UK. His prose work has been shortlisted for the Manchester Fiction Prize and has appeared in magazines like Storgy and Lunate. His short story/flash collection 'Flare and Falter' was published in 2019 by Splice, and longlisted for the Edge Hill Short Story Prize.

24. Nick Allen gets most of his sustenance from double espressos and malt whisky and after a lifetime of denial is finally willing to admit his poetry habit in public. He talks to poets in darkened rooms at the back of pubs and sometimes feels enlightened. Mainly he worries…

25. Rachel Burns was shortlisted in Wolves Poetry Lit Fest 2021 judged by Liz Berry and won second place in The Julian Lennon Prize For Poetry 2021. Her poetry pamphlet, A Girl in a Blue Dress, is published by Vane Women Press.

26. Sarah-Jane Crowson's work is inspired by fairytales, psychogeography and surrealism. She uses bricolage to investigate the unusual and surprising; exploring the space between real and imagined. She is an educator at Hereford College of Arts, and a postgraduate researcher at Birmingham City University, investigating ideas of the 'critical radical rural'. She has visual poetry published in journals such as Waxwing, Petrichor and Iron Horse Literary Review, and her haiku was shortlisted for the Haiku Foundation's 'Touchstone' awards in 2020. You can find her on Twitter @Sarahjfc.

27. Selma Carvalho is a British-Asian writer whose short stories have been listed or placed in numerous contests including Fish, Bath, London Short Story, Dinesh Allirajah prize and is the winner of Leicester Writes Short Story prize. Her collection of short stories was a final-

ist for the prestigious SI Leeds Literary Prize. Her debut novel shortlisted for the Mslexia Novella Prize, was published by Speaking Tiger, India, in 2021. She lives in London and is represented by the Ruppin Agency.

28. Thomas Lawrance lives in Ireland, where he writes fiction and performs stand-up comedy. His writing was recently shortlisted for the *Alpine Fellowship Writing Prize*, and he was a runner-up in the *Seán Ó Faoláin Short Story Competition*.

29. Tim Kiely is a criminal barrister and poet based in London. His work has appeared in 'Lunar Poetry', 'South Bank Poetry', 'Under the Radar' and 'Magma'. His debut pamphlet, 'Hymn to the Smoke', is published by Indigo Dreams.

30. Yuan Changming hails with Allen Yuan from [poetrypacific.blogspot.ca](poetrypacific.blogspot.ca). Credits include eleven Pushcart nominations besides appearances in *Best of the Best Canadian Poetry* (2008-17) & *BestNewPoemsOnline*, among nearly 1900 others. Recently, Yuan published his eleventh chapbook *Limerence*, and served on the jury for Canada's 44th National Magazine Awards (poetry category).

# About Fly on the Wall Press

A publisher with a conscience.
Publishing high quality anthologies on pressing issues, novels, short stories and poetry, from exceptional writers around the globe. Founded in 2018 by founding editor, Isabelle Kenyon.

## Some other publications:

*The Woman With An Owl Tattoo by Anne Walsh Donnelly*

*the sea refuses no river by Bethany Rivers*

*The Prettyboys of Gangster Town by Martin Grey*

*The Sound of the Earth Singing to Herself by Ricky Ray*

*Inherent by Lucia Orellana Damacela*

*Medusa Retold by Sarah Wallis*

*Pigskin by David Hartley*

*We Are All Somebody*

*Aftereffects by Jiye Lee*

*Someone Is Missing Me by Tina Tamsho-Thomas*

*Odd as F\*ck by Anne Walsh Donnelly*

*Muscle and Mouth by Louise Finnigan*

*Modern Medicine by Lucy Hurst*

*These Mothers of Gods by Rachel Bower*

*Sin Is Due To Open In A Room Above Kitty's by Morag Anderson*

*Fauna by David Hartley*

*How To Bring Him Back by Clare HM*

*Hassan's Zoo and A Village in Winter by Ruth Brandt*

*No One Has Any Intention of Building A Wall by Ruth Brandt*

*The House with Two Letter-Boxes by Janet H Swinney*

*The Guts of a Mackerel by Clare Reddaway*

*A Dedication To Drwoning by Maeve McKenna*

## Social Media:

@fly_press (Twitter) @flyonthewall_poetry (Instagram)

@flyonthewallpress (Facebook)

www.flyonthewallpress.co.uk